Walking

Healed

By

Shantel Ragsdale

Dedication

This book is lovingly dedicated to my late father, Donnie "Jerry" Blyther.

Your faith was steadfast, your strength unshakable, and your trust in God unwavering. You taught me what it truly means to believe—even when life feels uncertain—to stand firm and let faith lead the way.

Because of your example, I learned that trust in God is not just a phrase; it's a way of life. Your legacy of faith continues to live in me, guiding my steps and reminding me that with God, all things are possible. Sometimes, we even must learn to suffer well.

Weeping may endure for a night, but joy comes in the morning. (Psalm 30:5)

Thank you, Dad, for showing me how to walk by faith and not by sight.

Acknowledgment

First, all glory, honor, and praise belong to God—the Author and Finisher of my faith. Lord Jesus Christ, thank You for Your grace, Your mercy, and Your presence in every word written. Without You, this work would not exist. This is Your book. I acknowledge You as my Savior, my source, my strength, and my guide. Thank You for the strength to make it through the storms and for the courage to help other women make it through as well.

I extend my deepest gratitude to my family, especially my mom, for her unwavering love, prayers, and encouragement. Your support carried me through moments of doubt and reminded me who I was and whose I was.

To my precious son, Tyriq, thank you for being my joy, my motivation, and a constant reminder of God's goodness. Everything I do is out of love for you and for the future God has prepared for you.

I can't forget my sweet fur baby, Pepper, who has given me companionship, laughter, and unconditional love through the years.

To every woman who will hold this journal—thank you for your courage to seek more. More healing. More truth. More of God. It is my prayer that these pages draw you closer to a life-changing encounter with the Lord Jesus Christ.

Lastly, thank you to everyone who has prayed for me, cried with me, encouraged me, and believed in the calling God placed on my life. Your support has not gone unnoticed, and I am forever grateful.

With love and gratitude, *Shantel Ragsdale*

Table of Contents

Foreword

Storms

Not all storms come with severe weather alerts Sometimes they sneak up on you out of nowhere. All can be calm, then suddenly there is an extreme shift in the atmosphere. The moving in of dark, ominous clouds that usher in a still, unnatural silence. Before you have a chance to take cover or even take a breath, the winds begin to blow and the clouds burst, releasing a torrential downpour, making it impossible to recognize that which was once familiar. You begin to question everything—who you are, if you will make it through, and where God is in all of the devastation.

Well, let me tell you what I have learned. There is no panic button on God's throne. He is never taken off guard, nor is He intimidated by your pain and brokenness. He is not distant when you cry yourself to sleep at night; He is right there an ever -present help in a time of trouble (Psalm 46:1). And He is near to the brokenhearted and those who are crushed in spirit (Psalm 34:18). He will fix what you thought was unfixable, redeem what you thought was wasted, and restore what you thought you had lost forever. I know it to be true, because He has done it for me.

Walking Healed was birthed out of those sacred, silent places where I wrestled with God and eventually surrendered to His sovereign power. It's a journey that I'm still on—learning that healing is not a one-time event, but a daily choice, a daily journey. Some days you run, some days you walk, and some days you may even limp, but every step with God is a step forward.

This devotion is an invitation—a relatable guide to women everywhere who have walked through the fire and wonder if their burns will ever heal. It is for those who need to know that through God, healing is available; those who need to know that they are not alone or forgotten. Trust me when I tell you there is strength in the stretching-No matter how severe the storm, what you have lost can be restored. There is still life, love, and purpose on the other side of the pain.

My prayer for you is that after reading God's promises, believing the affirmations, and applying the scriptures in this devotion, you will no longer walk around wounded, you will Walk Healed!

With Grace, Peace, and Love,

Shantel

Pre-Journey Assessment: "Where Am I Right Now?"

On a scale of 1–10, rate how much peace you currently feel in each area:

- My relationship with God:

☐ 1 ☐ 2 ☐ 3 ☐ 4 ☐ 5 ☐ 6 ☐ 7 ☐ 8 ☐ 9 ☐ 10

- My emotional well-being:

☐ 1 ☐ 2 ☐ 3 ☐ 4 ☐ 5 ☐ 6 ☐ 7 ☐ 8 ☐ 9 ☐ 10

- My ability to forgive:

☐ 1 ☐ 2 ☐ 3 ☐ 4 ☐ 5 ☐ 6 ☐ 7 ☐ 8 ☐ 9 ☐ 10

- My self-worth:

☐ 1 ☐ 2 ☐ 3 ☐ 4 ☐ 5 ☐ 6 ☐ 7 ☐ 8 ☐ 9 ☐ 10

- My hope for the future:

☐ 1 ☐ 2 ☐ 3 ☐ 4 ☐ 5 ☐ 6 ☐ 7 ☐ 8 ☐ 9 ☐ 10

There is something about healing that's quiet.

It does not announce itself.

It just keeps happening.

- *Author Unknown*

Day 1

Day 1: I Am Not Broken Beyond Repair

Psalm 147:3 — He heals the brokenhearted and binds up their wounds.

Word of the day: Healing

Affirmation:

God is healing me from the inside out. I am whole in His perfect hands.

Devotion:

Some days, the ache can be so debilitating that you wonder if you'll ever be whole. God says you are not discarded; you are His beloved. He does not rush to put a bandage on your heart—He mends it with patience, presence, and love. Every tear that has formed and fallen, He has collected and counted. Let the comfort of His nearness, not your present pain, be the loudest truth that speaks to you today. Take a moment, set your affections on Him—the true lover of your soul. His love and strength endure forever, and His word will never fall to the ground. The Father wastes nothing; He can work out even the toughest and most painful seasons in your favor.

God has not forgotten, nor has He changed His perfect plan for your life. His love is unmatched, and there is safety in His embrace when you surrender all to Him.

Prayer:

Lord, gather every shattered place and bind it with Your love. Teach me to rest while You restore.

Journaling prompt: (feel free to create your own)

Write a short letter to yourself beginning with:

"Dear (me), even though I feel broken, I am still loved and being made whole."

Let the letter be gentle and honest.

Ask yourself Where do I still feel broken? What tender truth can I speak about that place today?

Acknowledge one area of pain that still feels raw, and then answer it with a truth from Psalm 147:3 —

"He heals the brokenhearted and binds up their wounds."

Close your letter with a statement of faith, such as:

"I am not beyond repair. Healing is already happening within me."

Acts of Self-Care:

Light a candle.

Inhale slowly through your nose for 4 seconds, hold your breath for 2 seconds, exhale through the mouth for 6 seconds.

With each breath, whisper a word from Psalm 147:3 — "He heals … the brokenhearted … and binds up their wounds."

Picture God knitting your heart gently with His love.

Stand in front of the mirror.

Look at the daughter of the Most High King looking back at you, and repeat:

"I am not beyond repair. God's hands are steady on my healing."

Suggested Worship Song:

He Knows My Name — Tasha Cobbs Leonard

Journal Entries

Day 2

Worthy of Love Again

Song of Solomon 4:7 — You are altogether beautiful, my darling; there is no flaw in you.

Word of the day: Worthy

Affirmation:

I am worthy of love, affection, and tenderness. I was never disqualified.

Devotion:

So often, past pain tries to coax you into self-protection. But Christ never stopped calling you worthy. His love teaches you how to receive again—slowly, safely, wisely. You don't have to audition for love when you are the beloved of Christ. Don't allow the emotional conflict of your past hurts to deceive you into believing that you are not good enough to be loved. - (You will hear me say many times during this journey) The devil is a liar! - he is the father of lies. Don't believe him.

Your Heavenly Father, who is Love, says that you are the apple of His eye according to Deuteronomy 32:10. Silence the lies of the enemy and know that you are not counted out. You are worthy of receiving and giving love.

Prayer:

God, restore my belief in love. - Help me cast down the negative stories I tell myself and replace them with Your truth. Amen.

Journaling prompt: (feel free to create your own)

Reflect on the beliefs you've carried regarding your worth.

> What past experiences or hurts have built these beliefs?

> How have these beliefs affected the way you perceive love in relationships?

> Now, open God's word from Song of Solomon 4:7 to rewrite these beliefs.

Act of Self-Care:

> Write what you choose to believe today from the Song of Solomon, think of how God sees you, and how He wants you to see yourself.

> Write this choice as a truth, an unquestioned fact:

> "I am worthy of love, affection, and tenderness. I am God's beloved, and His love is enough for me."

> Read the note aloud to yourself.

Suggested Worship:

> *Goodness of God* — Ce Ce Winans

Journal Entries

Day 3

Day 3: When Doubt Whispers, God Speaks

Zephaniah 3:17 — He will rejoice over you with singing.

Word of the day: Secure

Affirmation:

I silence self-doubt with the voice of God's truth. I am seen, loved, and delighted In.

Devotion:

It is so easy to get caught up in the web of lies that self-doubt weaves. It will make you insecure about your self-worth, abilities, and your future. The reality is that God has already spoken the truth over your life before the foundation of the world. Whenever doubt rises, remember that your Heavenly Father delights in you. Lean close to Him and let His love drown out all insecurity. Remember that the One who formed you still calls you wonderful. Where there is weakness, He offers strength. Where there is lack, He provides abundance, and in times of uncertainty, He offers reassurance. He has already gone before you to straighten your paths. So, lift your head, stare doubt in the face, and say, "I am God's beloved, and I am more than enough!"

Prayer:

Father, tune my heart to Your voice. Turn down the noise of shame and fear. Amen.

Journaling prompt:

Reflect on your feelings of uncertainty, doubt, and inadequacy.

Write out these doubts.

Now, write truths from God that negate these doubts, one by one.

Act of Self-Care:

Set a quiet space for yourself.

Put on worship music that invites peace and stillness (suggested: Lauren Daigle's "You Say").

Journal one thing that God delights in about you.

Consider His love for you, the way He formed you, or your ability to love others.

Write as though God Himself has spoken to you: "God delights in my…"

Read what you wrote aloud.

Suggested Worship:

You Say — Lauren Daigle

Journal Entries

Day 4

Day 4: Peace Be still.

Isaiah 26:3 (NIV) "You will keep in perfect peace those whose minds are steadfast, because they trust in You."

Word of the day: Peace

Affirmation:

I release anxiety and embrace the peace of God that steadies my soul.

Devotion: Peace is not the absence of problems—it is the presence of God in the middle of them. Life may swirl with uncertainty, and fear often comes knocking on the door of your mind. But peace is not something you have to chase. It is already yours in Christ Jesus.

When your heart feels restless, remember that peace begins with where you set your mind. Shift your focus from what you cannot control to the One who is in control. He is steady when you are shaken and constant when you feel tossed about. The peace of God is not fragile—it is strong enough to anchor you in the fiercest storm.

Prayer:

Lord, I surrender my worries and my restless thoughts to You. Fill my heart with Your peace that surpasses understanding. Help me trust You more deeply so that my mind stays fixed on You, not my fears.

Journaling prompt:

Reflect

In which areas of life have anxiety, worry, or fear been affecting you?

What concerns and worries have been stealing your peace?

Write down these worries and release them to God.

Shift your focus!

Write truths about God's sovereignty over you and your problems.

Write down one or two promises from Scripture (like Isaiah 26:3, Philippians 4:6–7, John 14:27) that calm your heart and mind.

Write a declaration of peace over the concerns you've written down.

For example:

"I release my worry about the future to God, for He holds tomorrow. I embrace His peace, knowing He is in control, and I can trust Him completely."

Act of Self-Love:

Steady your breath!

Sit comfortably in a quiet space.

Breathe in for 4 seconds, hold it for 2, and exhale for 6 seconds.

Repeat 3 times.

Feel God's peace surrounding you.

Hand your anxieties over to God.

Write down your troubles and worries on a small piece of paper.

Say out loud: *I surrender these to You, Lord. You are in control, and I trust You.*

Journal a Scripture on peace

Write any Scripture from Isaiah 26:3, John 14:27, or Philippians 4:6–7.

How does this Scripture speak to your current circumstances?

Write it on a card to keep in your pocket.

Speak it to yourself whenever you feel anxious.

Suggested Worship:

"Peace Be Still" –Lauren Daigle

Day 5

Day 5: The Courage to Feel Again

Ezekiel 36:26 — I will remove your heart of stone and give you a heart of flesh.

Word of the Day: Tenderness

Affirmation:

I am safe to feel again. God is softening what life tried to harden in my soul.

Devotion:

When you have been hurt deeply, your heart starts building walls quietly, silently, out of survival. In an effort to protect yourself- you stop expecting joy, but joy cannot reach a barricaded heart. You grow comfortable with numbness. But God never designed your heart to be hardened. He created it to feel and to love.

The courage to feel again doesn't mean you won't get hurt. It means you trust God enough to hold you when you do. Feeling is a sign of life. It's a reminder that the Spirit of God is still moving in you, still tenderizing the places where grief, betrayal, or disappointment tried to make you cold.

Let today be a turning point. Do not fear your tears or laughter—they are part of the healing. Invite God into every emotion, knowing that He will never waste a single feeling surrendered to Him. Invite God to soften the guarded places. Feeling again is not weakness; it's evidence of healing.

Prayer:

Lord, melt the ice around my heart. Teach me to feel without fear and to love without panic.

Journaling prompt:

Reflect

What emotions are you avoiding because of the hurt they carry? These might include sadness, anger, fear, or even joy.

Why do these emotions feel unsafe or difficult to experience? What is the "wall" you've built to protect yourself from these emotions?

Write these emotions and give them over to God in your journal:

"Lord, I hand over my fear of feeling to You. Soften the hardness in me. Help me trust You enough to allow myself to feel again. Let me truly believe that You will hold me through every emotion."

Write/Speak aloud!

"I am safe to feel again. God is softening what life tried to harden. His tenderness heals me."

Act of Self-Care:

Listen to a worship song (suggested: Come Alive (Dry Bones)) in a quiet place. Let yourself feel the song and the emotions it brings.

Name every emotion you feel while listening to the song.

Remember, by feeling, you are presenting every emotion to God. Prayerfully invite Him into these feelings.

Remind yourself that you are allowing the emotions to come back to your heart and body with God's help.

Suggested Worship:

Come Alive (Dry Bones)— Lauren Daigle

Journal Entries

Assessment

(Take a few quiet moments at the end of Day 5. Answer these questions honestly. There are no right or wrong answers — this is simply a snapshot of your thoughts and feelings after you have progressed this far.)

Emotional Awareness

1. What emotions do I feel most often these days (peace, sadness, anxiety, anger, numbness, joy)?

   ____

2. When was the last time I truly felt at peace with myself?

   ____

3. Are there emotions I've been avoiding or suppressing?

   ____

4. What situations or people most often trigger emotional pain or stress for me?

   ____

   ____

   ____

5. What does my heart needs healing from right now?

24

Day 6

Day 6: Beauty Beyond Scars

Isaiah 61:3 — To bestow on them a crown of beauty instead of ashes.

Word of the Day:

Beauty

Affirmation:

My scars tell a story of survival, not shame. God is turning my ashes into beauty.

Devotion:

 Heartbreak often makes everything feel final, but God is the God of restoration. He doesn't just mend what is broken— He transforms it into something beautiful. Your scars are not wasted; scar tissue is proof you lived through something and survived.

In God's hands, scars become evidence of His covering. So, hold on, because what feels like the end can become a beautiful beginning. Every scar can tell a story, not of disgrace but of God's grace.

Prayer:

Father, help me see beyond today-one day at a time, one step at a time, one prayer at a time. Turn my scars into testimonies that point to Your faithfulness. Use my story to reflect al scar still carries the weight of shame or pain?

Reflect on the story it tells. Was it a story of betrayal, heartbreak, or Your glory. Amen.

Journal prompt:

Reflect

Which physical, emotional, or relation grief?

Now, imagine how God might want you to see the story. Instead of viewing it as a reminder of defeat or shame, imagine how God intended it to be a tool of His grace, offering you survival and strength.

Create a new story for your scar:

What does it tell you about your strength or resilience?

How does it reflect God's restoration in your life?

Write your affirmation over it:

"My scars tell a story of survival, not shame. God is turning my ashes into beauty."

Act of Self-Care:

In a secluded place, choose a physical or emotional scar to focus on.

Place your hand on the scar or your heart, and speak aloud:

This scar is evidence of God's faithfulness during challenging times. I bless this scar, the resilience and healing it represents, and the strength it brought me.

Thank God for the healing, for the lessons you learned, and the strength you gained. Ask for His help in seeing your circumstances in a way that aligns with His mercy and grace for you.

Affirm: *I am more than my scars. I am a testament to God's grace and restoration.*

Suggested Worship:

Beauty for Ashes — Crystal Lewis

Journal Entries

Journal Entries

Day 7

Day 7: Learning to Trust Again

Proverbs 3:5-6 — Trust in the Lord with all your heart and lean not on your own understanding. Acknowledge Him, and He will direct your paths.

Word of the Day:

Trust

Affirmation:

I will keep my mind on Jesus and He will keep me in perfect peace.

Devotion:

Life doesn't always play out the way we expect. Doors close, relationships shift, and plans unravel. In those moments, our instinct is to demand answers to lean on our own understanding. But Proverbs reminds us: peace and direction come not from knowing everything, but from trusting the One who does. Trust is surrender. It is saying, "Lord, even though I don't see the way, I believe You are the Way." It is choosing faith when sight fails, confidence when doubt rises, and surrender when control slips through your fingers. Trust in God isn't passive—it is active faith, a daily decision to put your life, dreams, and healing in His hands. As you walk through your own journey of healing, remember: God's view is bigger than yours. He sees the whole picture, while you only see the puzzle piece. Trust does not erase the pain, but it transforms it, reminding you that God never wastes a tear and always weaves good from brokenness.

Prayer:

Father, today I surrender the pieces I do not understand. Please help me trust You even when I can't trace You. Calm my racing thoughts when doubt rises and remind me that You are directing my path. I don't need to see the whole picture—I just need to hold Your hand. Thank You for being steady when I feel shaken.

Journal prompt:

What is the situation in your life right now that feels hardest to trust God with?

How has God been faithful in the past that I can remember as a source of strength today?

Reflect on your fears and uncertainties about this situation. What makes you try to control it?

Pause for a moment to surrender this situation completely and intentionally to God.

Write down a prayer of surrender and trust:

"Lord, I may not understand the way, but I trust You. Direct my path even when I can't see the whole picture or the prize You've prepared for me and help me let go of my desire to control it."

Act of Self-Care:

Take a piece of paper and write down your uncertainties and worries-Place them in your Bible under

Jeremiah 29:11 to remind yourself of God's plan for you and His promise to prosper you and not to harm you.

Speak aloud "Lord, I surrender my worries to You. I don't need to see the whole picture. I choose to trust You with each worry."

Suggested Worship:

Trust in You — Lauren Daigle

Journal Entries

Day 8

Day 8: Rest for the Weary

Matthew 11:28 — Come to Me, all who are weary and burdened, and I will give you rest.

Word of the Day:

Rest

Affirmation:

I can come to Jesus and find true rest.

Devotion:

In a world that praises hustle and constant striving, rest can feel like weakness. But God calls you to a different rhythm. Healing requires rest. You cannot pour from an empty cup (I've tried), nor can your soul thrive when it is always running on empty. Yet so often we fill- our days with meaningless tasks just to avoid stillness, afraid that if we stop, the pain will catch up to us. But rest is where God meets you in your quiet place. When you stop striving, you make space for Him to whisper, "You are safe. You are loved. You are enough." True rest is not just physical; it is spiritual. It is laying down your need to be in control and allowing the Holy Spirit to lead you to quiet waters.

God never asked you to prove your worth by how much you accomplish. He asked you to abide, to rest in His presence, and to let His peace restore what the world has worn down. Rest in His loving embrace.

Prayer:

Father, I am tired: sometimes in my body, but more often in my soul. Teach me to rest in You, not just with my schedule, but with my heart. Help me to release the pressure I place on myself and find peace in Your promises.

Journal Prompt:

Write a gentle reflection beginning with:

"Dear God, I am tired, and this is where I feel the weight the most…"

Let yourself be honest without fixing anything.

Name what is exhausting you—not just physically, but emotionally and mentally.

Ask yourself:

What am I carrying that You never asked me to carry?

- *Where have I confused striving with worth?*

After naming the burden, respond to yourself with the truth of Matthew 11:28:

"Come to Me… and I will give you rest."

Close your entry with a sentence of surrender, such as:

"I do not have to earn rest. I am allowed to lay this down."

Act of Self-Care:

Thirty minutes before sleep, dim the lights and power down all devices.

Sit or lie comfortably and place one hand on your chest, one on your abdomen.

Breathe slowly—inhale for 4 counts, exhale for 6.

With each exhale, quietly release one word you associate with pressure (*prove, hurry, fix, control*).

Then whisper:

"Jesus, I come to You."

On the next breath:

"You give me rest."

Picture yourself setting down a heavy pack you've been carrying. You do not pick it back up tonight.

Before sleep, say aloud:

"Rest is not weakness. Rest is where I am restored."

Suggested Worship:

Breathe— Michael W. Smith

Journal Entries

Day 9

Day 9: Chosen and Cherished

1 Peter 2:9 (NIV) — "But you are a chosen people, a royal priesthood, a holy nation, God's special possession, that you may declare the praises of Him who called you out of darkness into His wonderful light."

Word of the Day:

Identity

Affirmation:

I am chosen by God, set apart for His glory, and cherished beyond measure.

Devotion:

Healing often reveals insecurities in us where we've felt overlooked or unwanted. But God's Word declares that you belong to Him. You are not here by chance; you were handpicked, intentionally created, and deeply loved. To be chosen is to be pursued, wanted, and claimed. To be cherished is to be valued, treasured, and held with care. God does both for you. When you forget your worth, remember the price He paid on the cross. When you doubt your value, remember the crown of life He promises.

You are not abandoned; you are adopted into His family. You are not forgotten; your name is written on His heart. You are not unloved; you are cherished with a love that will never let you go. The world will try to tell you that you're replaceable, forgettable, or not enough. But God's truth says otherwise—you are chosen, not as an afterthought, not by accident, but by divine design. And not only chosen but cherished—loved with an everlasting love that no failure, no rejection, no loss can erase.

Prayer:

Father, thank You for choosing me before I even chose You. Thank You for cherishing me, even when I struggle to cherish myself. Help me to walk in the confidence of Your love and to remember daily that I am treasured in Your sight.

Journaling Prompt:

Set a timer for **7 minutes** and write one honest page starting with:

"Today I forget I'm chosen and cherished when…"

Then answer these three lines (keep it simple and specific):

- **The old story I slip into is: "**______________**"** (ex: I'm not enough, I'm easy to replace, I don't matter)

- **The evidence from my real life that challenges that story is: "**_____________**"** (one trait, one moment, one way you've grown, one way you've loved well)

- **The truth I'm practicing today from 1 Peter 2:9 is:** "I belong to God, and my identity is not up for negotiation."

Close with one sentence:

"One way I'll act like I'm cherished today is _______________."

Act of Self-Care:

Write "I am chosen. I am cherished. I am loved." on a sticky note and place it where you'll see it every morning, on your mirror, your desk, or your journal. Speak it aloud each morning as a declaration of truth.

One boundary of self-respect today (1 step)

Pick one small action that treats you like someone valuable:

- say "not today" to one draining request.

- take a 10-minute quiet break.

- eat something nourishing.

- stop rereading a message that triggers you.

- speak to yourself the way you would speak to someone you love.

Suggested Worship:

How He Loves – John Mark McMillian

Day 10

Day 10: No Condemnation

Romans 8:1 — There is now no condemnation for those who are in Christ Jesus.

Word of the Day:

Freedom

Affirmation:

Shame has no authority over me; I am free in Christ.

Devotion:

Condemnation and shame love to show up uninvited, reminding you of failures and replaying painful moments. But those voices are not from God. He convicts to heal, not to condemn. Condemnation pushes you away from God; conviction gently draws you closer to Him. The enemy wants you stuck in the guilt of your past, so you will not step into your calling. But Christ wants you free. The same power that raised Him from the grave has broken the chains of shame in your life. You do not have to earn His love; it was already poured out on the cross. You do not need to hide your scars. They are proof that shame did not win, and condemnation did not have the final word.

Prayer:

Lord, thank You for setting me free from condemnation. Remind me, when shame whispers, that my past is forgiven and forgotten in Your sight. Let me walk in boldness, not fear, knowing I am loved, redeemed, and covered in Your grace. Amen

Journaling Prompt:

Set a timer for **6 minutes**. Keep it simple and direct.

Write this sentence and finish it honestly:

"The same story that keeps replaying in my mind is…"

Then write three short lines:

- **What it is trying to make me believe about me is:** "________________"

- **What I would say to a friend who felt this way is:** "________________"

- **What I'm choosing to answer it with today (Romans 8:1) is: "There is no condemnation for me in Christ. I can learn, repent, and move forward."**

Close with one action you'll take from freedom, not fear:

"Today I will ________________ (one small step)."

Act of Self-Care:

Stand in front of the mirror. Put one hand on your chest (this helps your nervous system settle). Breathe slowly.

Say out loud, steady and calm:

"I am free. I am forgiven. I am not condemned. God loves me."

Make it practical (so it lands, not just sounds good)
After you say it, add one sentence that names growth:

"I can take responsibility without punishing myself."

Then do one small "clean next step" right away (pick one):

- write a short apology or repair text (if appropriate)

- delete one screenshot/message you keep rereading to punish yourself.

- write one lesson learned in your notes.

- do a 5-minute tidy of your space as a reset signal.

- take a short walk and let the moment pass without arguing with it.

Suggested Worship:

No Condemnation- Anthony Edwards

Journal Entries

Assessment

(Take a few quiet moments at the end of Day 5. Answer these questions honestly. There are no right or wrong answers — this is simply a snapshot of your thoughts and feelings after you have progressed this far.)

Spiritual Connection

6. How close do I currently feel to God?

____

____

7. When I pray or worship, what do I most often feel — connection, distance, guilt, comfort, or confusion?

____

____

8. What is one area of my faith I struggle to trust God in?

____

____

9. How does God sees me at this moment in my life?

____

____

10. Is there a promise in Scripture that feels hard for me
    to believe?

Day 11

Day 11: The Shepherd's Care

Psalm 23:1 — The Lord is my Shepherd; I shall not want.

Word of the Day:

Provision

Affirmation:

The Father tends to me with His loving care; I lack nothing-.

Devotion:

Life is so often uncertain, and it is at those times fear screams the loudest: "What if what I have isn't enough? What if I am not enough?" But God's Word reminds us that He is a God of more than enough. God is never caught off guard; He sees your needs long before you tell Him. He is not careless with your heart or blind to the trials you face. His provision isn't limited to finances; it covers your emotions, your healing, and even your relationships. Whether you need strength for today, hope for tomorrow, or resources in your time or season of lack, He promises to provide, and His Word never fails. You are not forgotten, and you will not be forsaken. He is Jehovah Jireh, the God who provides.

Remember, provision isn't always about giving you everything you want, but it is always about giving you everything you need. Sometimes His provision comes in unexpected ways—a kind word, unexpected strength, the generosity of a stranger, or the opening of doors that would otherwise have been closed.

Prayer:

Father, thank You for being Jehovah Jireh, my Provider. Please remind me that I do not have to live in fear of lack, because in Psalm 84:11 it says, "No good thing does God withhold from those who walk upright." My Lord, help me to trust that You see every need and will meet it in Your perfect timing. Amen.

Journaling Prompt:

Set a timer for **7 minutes**.

Write this sentence and finish it clearly: **"The place I feel lack the most right now is…"**

Then answer these three quick lines:

- **What I am afraid will happen if this doesn't get provided is: "________________"**

- **What I actually need (not what I wish) in this season is: "______________"** (support, stability, rest, clarity, courage, money plan, connection)

- **One way God has already provided for me before is: "______________"** (a person, a door opening, strength you didn't expect, a timely resource)

Close with one grounding truth from Psalm 23:1:

"The Lord is my Shepherd; I shall not want. I can take the next step without panic."

Act of Self-Care:

Lack-to-plan practice (5 minutes)

1. On a small card or sticky note, write the one area you feel you are lacking.

2. Write over it in bold: **"God will provide."**

3. Under that, add **one practical next step** you can take today (keep it small):

- ask one person for help or advice.

- make a short budget/checklist.

- schedule one appointment

- send one follow-up message.

- set one boundary that protects your energy.

Carry the note with you or place it where you will see it.

Each time you notice fear rising, read the bold line once, then do (or schedule) the **one next step**—this trains your brain to move from scarcity panic to steady action.

Suggested Worship:

Jireh — Elevation Worship & Maverick City Music

Day 12

Day 12: Peace in the Storm

Philippians 4:6-7 — The peace of God... will guard your heart and mind in Christ Jesus.

Word of the Day:

Calm

Devotion:

Storms will come, but they are no match for the peace found in Jesus. It is easy to sing worship songs and evangelize about God's goodness when everything is calm. But when the storm rages, that's when peace feels farthest away. Jesus never promised a storm-free life, but He did promise to be with you in each storm. True peace isn't about everything being a walk in the park or making sense; it's about knowing Who is in the boat with you. Peace is not always found in the absence of the storm—it is found in the presence of Jesus.

Affirmation:

I release anxiety and receive God's guarding peace.

Prayer is the doorway from panic to peace. Make your request to the Lord and trust that He is El Roi, the God who sees.

Prayer:

Father, You are the Prince of Peace. Please calm my mind and guard my heart. Jehovah-Shammah, be with me when the chaos of life seems too much to bear and let me remember that You are always in control.

Journaling Prompt:

Write one anxious thought exactly as it shows up in your mind:

"Right now I'm anxious that __________________."

Then turn it into a simple prayer sentence (same topic, softer grip):

"God, I feel anxious about ________________. Please guard my heart and mind and help me take the next right step."

Finish with one practical grounding line:

"The next right step I can take in the next 24 hours is _________________."

Act of Self-Care:

15-minute calm reset (no phone)

Set a timer for **15 minutes** and sit in silence.

1. **Breathe to settle your body**

   Inhale 4 seconds, hold 2, exhale 6. Repeat for 2 minutes.

2. **Name what's happening (reduces overwhelm)**

   Quietly label it: **"This is anxiety. This is a storm moment."**

3. **Let peace "guard" your mind (mental boundary)**

When thoughts surge, don't argue with them. Just return to one phrase:

"Guard my heart and mind." (Philippians 4:6–7)

End with one gentle action

When the timer ends, do one calming, body-based step: drink water, stretch your shoulders, or take a short walk—something that tells your system, **"I'm safe enough to continue."**

Suggested Worship:

Peace Be Still— Lauren Daigle

Day 13

Day 13: Hope and a Future

Jeremiah 29:11 (NIV) — "'For I know the plans I have for you,' declares the Lord, 'plans to prosper you and not to harm you, plans to give you hope and a future.'"

Word of the Day:

Hope

Affirmation:

God's plans for me are good; I lean into His future with courage.

Devotion:

When life feels uncertain, it's easy to wonder if your past choices have caused you to miss out on your blessings. Please know that God has not changed His plan for your life, and His promises will never expire. He does not change like the seasonsHe is faithful.

Your future is not defined by your current circumstances but by His promises. Jeremiah 29:11 wasn't written in a time of joy and peace; God was speaking to people living in exile, far from what they hoped for. The Scripture was meant to remind them that no matter how dark things may look, their future rests in the hands of a faithful, loving God. No matter where you are in your life, God has a plan—and although you may not be able to see past the pain of today, our Heavenly Father is a redeemer. Deliverance is available for those who trust Him.

Prayer:

Father, thank You for giving me hope and a future. Remind me that no setback, delay, or disappointment can cancel Your plans for me. Teach me to trust in Your perfect timing and have faith in the path You have laid.

Journal Prompt:

Write this sentence and finish it honestly:

"If I truly believed God has good plans for me, today I would..."

Then write three quick lines:

- **One fear that makes me think the future won't work out is: "_______________"**

- **A more balanced thought I can practice (Jeremiah 29:11) is:** "God can work with my story. I'm not behind beyond repair."

- **One small action I can take today that matches hope is: "_______________"**

(Example: send one email, take one walk, apply once, clean one corner, ask for help, rest without guilt.)

Close with:

"Hope isn't denial. It's choosing the next step while God holds the bigger plan."

Act of Self-Care:

On paper, write **three hopes**—small, medium, and big (keep them real and simple):

1. **A small hope for this week:** __________

2. **A medium hope for this season:** __________

3. **A big hope for my future:** __________

Next to each one, write one **next-right-step** you can do within **48 hours** (tiny is fine).

Then pray one sentence:

"God, I place these in Your hands. Guide my steps and steady my heart."

Finish by writing:

"I will not abandon my future today."

Suggested Worship:

See a Victory — Elevation Worship

Day 14

Day 14: A New Thing

Isaiah 43:19 (NIV) – "See, I am doing a new thing! Now it springs up; do you not perceive it? I am making a way in the wilderness and streams in the wasteland."

Word of the Day:

Renewal

Affirmation:

I welcome God's new thing and release the old.

Devotion:

Sometimes renewal starts within the heart before it's visible in our circumstances. It rises up in those barren, dry places where nothing seems to grow. But a single touch from God can make streams flow, turning your wasteland into a beautiful garden. Letting go of the old is not always easy, but sometimes we hold on so tightly that we cannot receive the new thing that God wants to give us. Don't mourn closed doors; watch for new paths in the wilderness. Renewal requires a great deal of trust and a willingness to let go of past hurts or insecurities. I believe that God is doing a new thing in you right now. Open your heart and receive it!

Prayer:

Way Maker, open my eyes to the new You're growing. Teach me to release the old patterns, old wounds, and old fears so I can embrace the renewal You've promised. Make streams of life flow into every dry place within me.

Journal Prompt:

Write one clear line:

"The old pattern I'm ready to release is _________________."

Then answer these three practical prompts:

- **When it shows up, it usually gets triggered by:**
"_________________"

- **It protects me by (even if it's unhealthy):**
"_________________" (control, numbing, overworking, withdrawing, people-pleasing)

- **The "new thing" I want to practice instead is:**
"_________________" (one specific behavior or mindset)

Close with one sentence tied to Isaiah 43:19:

"God is making a way for me. My next small step into the new is _________________."

Act of Self-Care:

Take a short walk outside with **no phone in your hand** (silence is fine).

1. **Use your senses to come back to the present**

   Name quietly: **5 things you see, 4 you feel, 3 you hear, 2 you smell, 1 you taste.**

   (This calms the nervous system and interrupts looping thoughts.)

2. **Pick one "new" cue from nature**

A leaf moving, a flower, fresh air, light on the ground—choose one and let it be your anchor.

3. **Say one simple truth while you walk**

"God is doing a new thing in me, even if it's not fully visible yet."

4. **Finish with one release action**

When you get home, do one small "letting go" step:

- delete one draft you keep rewriting from fear

- put one worry on paper and close the notebook

- clear one surface

Small releases make room for real renewal.

Suggested Worship:

A New Thing - Madison Ryann Ward

Journal Entries

Day 15

Day 15: The Beauty of Surrender **Word of the Day:**

Surrender

1 Peter 5:6 (NIV) — "Humble yourselves, therefore, under God's mighty hand, that He may lift you up in due time."

Affirmation:

Surrender is not defeat; it is freedom. I trust God enough to place every part of my life into His hands.

Devotion:

We often fight to hold on to control, believing that we have the power to protect ourselves by holding on to the steering wheel of life to alter the outcome of our situations. But true freedom is found not in grasping the wheel, but in surrender. God is not asking you to give up; He's asking you to hand over the heavy things you were never meant to carry.

Surrender is one of the most courageous acts of faith. It means releasing your grip on your plans, your timelines, and your outcomes, and placing them into the hands of the One who knows the end from the beginning.

It's not easy. Our hearts want to cling tightly to what we can see, feel, or touch—even when it's breaking us. But surrender is where healing begins. When you stop striving to fix everything yourself, you open the door for God to step in with His perfect plan.

Remember Jesus in Gethsemane, whispering, "Not my will, but Your will be done" (Luke 22:42). That surrender led to resurrection. And the same is true in your life—when you surrender, God brings new life, strength, and victory.

Prayer:

Lord, I release my fears, my future, and my failures into Your hands. Teach me to surrender daily, knowing You always have my good in mind. Lift me in Your timing and strengthen me in Your peace.

Write the sentence:

"The area of my life I'm still trying to control is…"

Then answer these three quick prompts:

- **Why does it feel hard to surrender this area?**

(Example: fear, pride, past hurt, insecurity)

- **What would it look like to fully surrender this area to God today?**

- **How would my heart feel if I let go of control in this area?**

Close with:

"Surrender is not giving up; it's trusting God's timing and plan for me."

Act of Self-Love:

Write down three things you're holding onto tightly (worry, plans, past mistakes, control over outcomes).

Pray over each one:

- "God, I give this to You because I can't carry it anymore."

- "Thank You for being the One who carries my burdens."

Fold the paper and place it in your Bible or a personal space as a **reminder**:

"God is in control, not me."

Release the grip physically—take one small action that represents your surrender:

- take a deep breath and let go of tension

- close a book or email you've been clinging to for reassurance

- say "no" to a decision that's been weighing on you

This small release opens the door for peace and trust.

Suggested Worship:

I Surrender All – CeCe Winans

Journal Entries

Assessment

(Take a few quiet moments at the end of Day 5. Answer these questions honestly. There are no right or wrong answers — this is simply a snapshot of your thoughts and feelings after you have progressed this far.)

Self-Perception

11. How do I describe myself in one sentence?

____

12. What do I believe about my worth or value?

____

13. Are there negative words I've allowed others to define me with?

____

____

14. What do I wish I could change about how I see myself?

____

____

____

____

15. What would "healed and whole" look like for me
    personally?

68

Day 16

Day 16: Faith Over Fear

2 Timothy 1:7 (NKJV) – "For God has not given us a spirit of fear, but of power and of love and of a sound mind."

Word of the Day:

Faith

Affirmation:

I will not allow fear to rule my life. God has given me power, love, and a sound mind.

Devotion:

will always try to take over when you're stepping into healing or walking into unknown territory. But God didn't create fear to rule your heart and mind; He is a God of peace. He gave you faith as a weapon. Fear plants seed of doubt to root in you. What could go wrong? God has already placed a garden of faith in you to show you the beauty of Him who never fails.

Fear has a way of paralyzing us, whispering that we aren't enough, that the future is uncertain, or that the past will repeat itself. But Scripture reminds us that fear does not come from God. What He gives instead is power to stand, love to cover, and peace to calm the storms that rage within.

Every time fear knocks, you have a choice: open the door or speak the truth over it. Faith doesn't deny fear is real; however, it does refuse to let fear have the final say. When you trust that God is with you, even in the unknown, fear loses its grip. Faith is not the absence of fear, but the decision to move on with God despite it. And each step you take in faith builds strength, confidence, and courage for the journey ahead.

Prayer:

Lord, please forgive me for the times that I have allowed fear to rule my heart. Today, I chose faith over fear. Fill me with courage to walk boldly in Your promises, trusting that You are with me even when I walk blind. Amen.

Journal Prompt:

Write this sentence and finish it:

"The fear that holds me back the most is…"

Then answer these three practical prompts:

- **What's the worst-case scenario that fear is showing me?**

- **What truth from God's Word can I replace that fear with?**

- **What's one small step I can take today to choose faith over fear?**

Close with:

"Faith doesn't mean fear isn't there, it means I choose to walk despite it."

Act of Self-Love:

Write down one fear you're currently struggling with.

Pray over it:

- o "God, I surrender this fear to You. I choose faith today. Please fill me with Your peace."

Replace fear with truth: Write a scripture or positive affirmation that combats this fear. For example:

- o *"I have power, love, and a sound mind."* (2 Timothy 1:7)

- o *"God is with me. I will not fear."*

Take one small step:

- o Acknowledge the fear, then do something you've been avoiding because of it. It could be sending an email, making a phone call, or simply choosing peace in a small moment.

- o Every step taken in faith builds confidence and courage.

Keep the note with you as a reminder that **faith moves even when fear is present**.

Suggested Worship:

"Fear Is Not My Future" – Maverick City Music & Kirk Franklin

Journal Entries

Day 17

Day 17: Overflowing Hope

Romans 15:13 (NIV) – "May the God of hope fill you with all joy and peace as you trust in Him, so that you may overflow with hope by the power of the Holy Spirit."

Word of the Day:

Hope

Affirmation:

My hope is overflowing because it rests in Jesus.

Devotion:

When God is the source of your hope, it doesn't just stay within you; it spills over into every area of your life, creating a torch that cannot be dimmed, and that light inspires those around you.

The world we live in today tries to drain us of every ounce of hope we possess. Bad news, disappointments, and delays can make you feel like hope is slipping away. But hope in God is something altogether different. It doesn't fade away when life is hard. Instead, it grows, multiplies, and overflows by the power of our Helper, the Holy Spirit.

Overflowing hope means it's not just enough for you, but it becomes a blessing for others as well. When you cling to the promises of God in the middle of uncertainty, your faith encourages others to believe again. When you choose joy despite the pain, your life becomes a testimony of hope for the world to see.

Your hope doesn't depend on circumstances; it depends on Christ. And in Him, your hope will never be put to shame (Romans 5:5). Let your cup overflow with hope until it touches everyone around you.

Prayer:

Father, please fill me with Your joy and peace so that my hope may spill over onto everyone I meet. Let my life reflect the hope I have in You. If I begin to allow doubt to creep in, remind me that You are the God of hope, and Your Word will never come back to You void.

Journal Prompt:

Write the sentence and finish it:

"The area where I need God to restore my hope today is..."

Then answer these three quick questions:

- **What circumstances are making this area feel hopeless?**

- **What truth from God's Word can I hold onto in this moment?**

- **How would my perspective shift if I believed that hope is always available in Jesus?**

Close with:

"My hope is anchored in Christ, and because of Him, I can trust for the overflow."

Act of Self-Love:

Write down three ways God has been faithful in your life—small or large moments that remind you of His consistency and goodness.

Keep this list visible: Place it somewhere you can see it often as a daily reminder of His faithfulness (on your desk, next to your bed, in your planner).

When doubt creeps in, read through the list and pray:

- "God, You have been faithful before, and I trust You will be again."

Share your hope: Reach out to one person today (through text, a call, or in person) and share a small testimony of God's faithfulness or encouragement. Let your hope overflow into their life as well.

Hope isn't just for you—it's meant to spill over into others.

Suggested Worship:

"Anchor" – Hillsong Worship

Journal Entries

Day 18

Day 18: Clothed in Strength

Proverbs 31:25 (NIV) – "She is clothed with strength and dignity; she can laugh at the days to come."

Word of the Day:

Strength

Affirmation:

I am clothed in God's strength and walk with dignity. My future is secure in His hands, and I face it with joy.

Devotion:

Most of us have a misconception about what it means to be strong. Strength is not about carrying heavy loads or having it all together; it's about leaning on the One who holds you together. His strength is made perfect in our weakness (2 Corinthians 12:9–11). When you are clothed in God's strength, you allow Him to uphold you with His hand. On the contrary, the world tells women that being strong means being relentless and unbreakable. That's why so many of us are stretched so thin and have no time to really seek God's guidance.

Scripture says you are clothed with strength and dignity. Being clothed in strength allows you to laugh at the days to come—not because life is always easy, but because you know Who holds your tomorrow.

Prayer:

Father, thank You for clothing me in strength and dignity. When I feel weak, remind me that Your power is alive within me. Help me to walk with confidence, trusting that my future is in Your hands.

Journal Prompt:

Write the sentence and finish it: **"I define strength as…"**

Then answer these three quick prompts:

- **How have I been trying to be strong on my own recently?**

- **What would it look like to rely on God's strength instead?**

- **How would my confidence shift if I fully trusted that God is holding my future?**

Close with:

"God's strength in me is perfect, and I can face the future with confidence."

Act of Self-Love:

Stand in front of the mirror and look at yourself directly in the eyes.

Declare out loud:

- "I am clothed in God's strength. I am filled with dignity. I am unshaken because my life is in His hands."

Breathe deeply and feel the weight of this truth settle in your body.

Take one action today that reflects God's strength within you:

- o Stand firm in a decision, let go of unnecessary stress, or prioritize something that renews your strength (like a quiet moment of rest, prayer, or saying no to an extra task).

Carry this confidence with you today, knowing that God's strength is holding you steady in every moment.

Your strength is not based on what you can do alone, but on the One who sustains you.

Suggested Worship:

"His Strength Is Perfect" – Ce Ce Winans

Day 19

Day 19: Anchored in His Love

Jeremiah 31:3 (NIV) – "I have loved you with an everlasting love; I have drawn you with unfailing kindness."

Word of the Day:

Love

Affirmation:

God's love is my anchor. Nothing can separate me from His perfect love.

Devotion:

An anchor doesn't stop the waves from coming, but it keeps the ship from drifting away from safety. In that same way, God's love won't always stop the storm, but it will keep you from being consumed by it. His unfailing love secures your soul, reminding you that no matter how strong the winds blow, you are safe in His hands. When you're anchored, storms may shake you, but they cannot break you. Remember that you are loved, seen, and cherished by a God who will never let you go.

Healing requires a safe place to anchor your soul, and nothing provides more safety than the love of Jesus. His love doesn't waver when you fail, it doesn't fade when you stumble, and it doesn't depend on your performance.

Prayer:

Father, let me never forget that Your love is the anchor of my life. Root me in the truth of who I am in You—chosen, cherished, and deeply loved.

Journaling Prompt:

Write the sentence and finish it: **"The love of God means to me…"**

Then answer these three prompts:

- **How have I experienced God's love as my anchor in the past?**

- **What makes it hard for me to believe that His love is unchanging?**

- **How would my choices today be different if I truly lived anchored in His love?**

Close with:

"No matter the storm, I am anchored in God's unchanging love."

Act of Self-Love:

Wrap yourself in a blanket, close your eyes, and imagine it as God's arms holding you tightly.

Breathe deeply, visualizing His love pouring over you with each breath.

Declare quietly to yourself:

o   "I am loved, seen, and cherished by God. His love holds me steady, no matter what."

Sit in stillness for a few moments, allowing the peace of being anchored in His love to wash over you.

Take one small, confident step today that reflects your security in God's love:

o   It might be a decision you've been hesitant about or a moment where you choose peace over fear.

Let this simple, calming practice remind you that you are always anchored in His love—no storm can take that away.

Suggested Worship:

"My Soul Has Been Anchored in the Lord" –

Douglas Miller

Journal Entries

Day 20

Day 20: For Her – Joy Comes in the Morning

Psalm 30:5 (NKJV) – "Weeping may endure for a night, but joy comes in the morning."

Word of the Day:

Joy

Affirmation:

My sorrow is temporary. God is faithful to bring me joy.

Devotion:

Pain may seem like it will last forever, but it never has the final say. God promises that morning will bring joy. There are seasons where the darkness seems so long and grief feels never-ending. But God assures us that joy is not gone—it is only waiting to show its face again so that healing can begin.

Healing doesn't erase your tears but take my word—it transforms them into a testimony of God's mercy and faithfulness. Every morning you open your eyes is proof that God isn't finished with you yet. The sun rising over your life is a reminder that hope is alive and joy is possible again.

This doesn't mean that the enemy won't try to steal your joy by pressing play on the slideshow of yesterday's pain, but you have the power to pull down imaginations and every high thing that exalts itself against the knowledge of God, bringing every thought into the obedience to Christ.

Prayer:

Lord, thank You that joy always follows sorrow. Help me to hold on through the hard seasons, trusting that Your light is on the way.

Journaling Prompt:

Write the sentence and finish it:

"The sorrow I am ready to surrender to God today is…"

Then answer these three prompts:

- **What is the pain or grief that feels overwhelming right now?**

- **How can I remind myself that joy is coming, even in this season?**

- **What evidence of God's faithfulness have I already seen in my life?** (Think of a past sorrow turned to joy, or a moment where God showed up.)

Close with:

"Though sorrow may last for the night, joy is always on the horizon."

Act of Self-Love:

Choose one thing that brings lightness to your heart—this might be listening to an uplifting song, dancing around your room, or laughing with a friend or loved one.

Give yourself permission to feel joy without guilt. Let yourself experience lightness, even if just for a few minutes.

Affirm joy over sorrow: Say aloud, **"Joy is coming, and I am open to receiving it now."**

Reflect on one thing in your life right now that you're grateful for—this gratitude is part of the joy God promises to bring, even in hard seasons.

Allow yourself to enjoy these moments of lightness, trusting that healing and joy are on the way.

Suggested Worship:

"Joy" – Housefires

Journal Entries

Assessment

(Take a few quiet moments at the end of Day 5. Answer these questions honestly. There are no right or wrong answers — this is simply a snapshot of your thoughts and feelings after you have progressed this far.)

Relationships and Boundaries

16. Are there people I need to forgive — including myself?

____

____

17. Which relationships in my life feel life-giving, and which feel draining?

____

____

18. Do I struggle to say no or set boundaries when I need to?

____

19. Is there someone whose approval I've been seeking instead of God's?

____

20. What relationship pattern keeps repeating that I want to break during this journey?

Day 21

Day 21: Day 21: – In His Perfect Timing

Ecclesiastes 3:1 (NIV) – "There is a time for everything, and a season for every activity under the heavens."

Word of the Day:

God's Timing

Affirmation:

I will not rush ahead or lag. Behind. I trust God's timing for every detail of my life.

Devotion:

This is something that I have personally struggled with in my life. Waiting is hard. We need everything microwaved! We want answers now, healing now, breakthrough now. But by now, I'm sure you have realized that healing is not instant and promises are not always fulfilled overnight. There are times when it feels like nothing is changing, but God is still working behind the scenes. His timing is not a delay or denial; it is preparation.

When we rush ahead of God's process, we may miss His blessing. But when you trust His divine timing, you begin to see that every season—both the waiting and the breakthrough—has a purpose. God's timing is never late. He knows the right season for every step of your journey, and His plan is worth the wait.

Even in seasons of stillness, God is shaping you. He is strengthening your faith, deepening your trust, and ordering your steps with His perfect will. Nothing is ever wasted in His hands.

Prayer:

Lord, thank You that Your timing is perfect. Forgive me for the times I've been impatient or anxious. Help me to rest in the knowledge that You are working all things together for my good, in Your perfect season. Amen.

Journaling Prompt:

Write the sentence and finish it:

"The area of my life where I'm struggling to wait on God's timing is..."

Then answer these three prompts:

- **What makes me anxious about waiting in this area?**

- **What truth from Scripture helps me trust in God's perfect timing?** (e.g., Ecclesiastes 3:1)

- **How can I shift my perspective today to rest in His timing instead of rushing ahead?**

Close with:

"I trust God's perfect timing for every detail of my life, and I choose to wait with peace."

Act of Self-Love:

Choose one task that feels rushed and put it aside for now.

Take a moment to pause and breathe deeply. Close your eyes for 2-3 minutes, focusing on the breath and reminding yourself:

"I am on God's timetable, not my own."

Reflect on a past season when God's timing worked out better than your own plans. Feel gratitude for that moment and trust that He is doing the same now.

Slow down your pace today by intentionally focusing on one small step or task at a time. Let go of the urgency and trust that His perfect plan is unfolding in every moment.

Taking these small, mindful pauses today helps you rest in the peace of knowing God's timing is always perfect.

Suggested Worship:

"Wait on You" – Elevation Worship and Maverick City Music

Journal Entries

Day 22

Day 22: Cast Your Cares

1 Peter 5:7 – Cast all your anxiety on Him because He cares for you.

Word of the Day:

Cares

Affirmation:

I do not carry my burdens alone. I release my cares into God's hands.

Devotion:

Life can pile up worries until you feel like you're carrying a backpack too heavy for your soul. Some burdens you share with others, but some you keep hidden deep inside. Yet God's Word is clear: cast it all on Him.

The weight you feel today was never meant for you to carry alone. God doesn't just see your burdens; He invites you to hand over every care, every fear, every anxious thought, and place them at His feet. And Leave Them There.

The word "casting" means throwing, not gently placing or holding on to. It's an act of releasing something that you should not be holding on to, trusting that the One who loves you will hold what you cannot.

When you release your care, you make space for His perfect peace. When you surrender your worries to Him, you open the door for His provision. Carrying them alone leaves you weary and bound; casting them on Him leaves you free.

Remember, He cares for you. Not in a general or distant sense, but personally and intimately, for eternity. The same God who created the universe holds your heart. What a blessing!

Prayer:

Lord, today I choose to cast every care upon You because You care for me. Take my fears, my stress, my anxiety, and my worries. Replace them with Your peace that surpasses all understanding. Thank You for loving me unconditionally. Amen.

Journaling Prompt:

With a 6-minute timer in place, write this sentence and finish it honestly:

"The worries I keep carrying in my body and mind are…"

Then answer these three short lines:

- **The cost of holding onto these worries is:** (sleep, tension, irritability, exhaustion, distraction)

- **What I can control about this situation is:** "________________"

- **What I cannot control—and need to release—is:** "________________"

Close with one grounding truth tied to 1 Peter 5:7:

"I am allowed to release what is too heavy for me. God can hold what I cannot."

Act of Self-Love:

Write your top three worries—one per line. Be specific.

Read them once, then say out loud:

"These are real concerns, but I do not have to carry them alone."

Crumple the paper and throw it away (or tear it up slowly).

As you do, say:

"I release this into God's care."

Reset your body

Take three slow breaths. Drop your shoulders. Unclench your jaw.

Choose one small action that supports peace today:

- step outside for fresh air

- drink a full glass of water

- write one next step for tomorrow

- stop researching or ruminating for the day

This trains your mind and body to practice **release instead of rumination**—again and again.

Suggested Worship:

"*Cast My Cares*" – Finding Favor

Day 23

Day 23: God's Faithfulness

Lamentations 3:22–23 (ESV) – "The steadfast love of the Lord never ceases; His mercies never come to an end; they are new every morning; great is Your faithfulness."

Word of the Day:

Faithful

Affirmation:

God is faithful to His Word. God has never failed me, and He never will. His faithfulness is my foundation.

Devotion:

Sometimes it's hard to see God's faithfulness in the moment, especially when prayers seem unanswered or when pain feels like it has no end. But when you look back, you'll notice His hand in your situation—providing, protecting, and guiding you every step of the way, even when you didn't realize it. The Father is consistent. Life may change, people may change, but God never changes. His faithfulness is the one thing that is certain in every season of your life— through joy, through sadness, through waiting, through trial, and through victory. Our God will not change.

His mercies are not recycled; they are new every morning. That means no matter what happened yesterday, today you wake up to fresh grace.

Faithfulness is not just something God does; it's who He is. He cannot deny Himself. If He promised to carry you,

He will. If He promised to heal you, He will. If He promised to love you forever, He already does. You don't need a miracle—all you need is a memory.

Prayer:

Lord, thank You for being faithful in every season of my life. When I forget, remind me of how You've already carried me through. Help me to live with confidence, knowing You will never leave me or forsake me. Amen.

Journalig Prompt:

Use rite this sentence and finish it:

"When I look back, one moment where I was carried—even if I didn't realize it then—was…"

Then write two short lines:

- **What I learned about myself or life through that moment is: "______________"**

- **The situation I'm facing right now that needs that same faithfulness is: "______________"**

Close with this grounding statement (linking memory to the present):

"God has been faithful before. I can allow that evidence to steady me today."

Act of Self-Love:

On paper, draw a simple vertical line.

Along the line, write **3–5 moments** where you made it through something hard:

- o   a season you survived

- o   help that showed up unexpectedly

- o   strength you didn't think you had

- o   a door that opened later than you wanted, but still opened

You don't need dramatic miracles—**ordinary survival counts.**

Circle one moment and write beside it:

"This proves I was not abandoned."

Place the paper somewhere you can return to it.

When doubt shows up, read it once and remind yourself:

"New mercy doesn't mean I forgot yesterday—it means I'm allowed to continue today."

This trains your mind to anchor in **evidence, not emotion**, while still honoring the spiritual truth of God's faithfulness.

Suggested Worship:

"Great Is Thy Faithfulness" – CeCe Winans

Journal Entries

Day 24

Day 24: A Renewed Mind

Romans 12:2 (NIV) – "Do not conform to the pattern of this world but be transformed by the renewing of your mind. Then you will be able to test and approve what God's will is, good, pleasing, and perfect will."

Word of the Day:

Renew

Affirmation:

I will renew my mind daily by reading the Word of God.

Devotion:

I think differently, live differently, and love differently because of His Spirit that lives in me.

Joyce Meyer wrote an amazing book entitled The Battlefield of the Mind. After reading it for the first time, I realized that healing must begin in my mind. The way you think about yourself, your past, and your future shapes the way you live and the choices you make. God offers you something greater than old thought patterns. He offers transformation through the renewing of the mind. Your thoughts have power because they become your words, and your words become your actions. They can either anchor you in truth or make you a slave to lies. The enemy loves to plant lies in our hearts to take root, therefore producing seeds of fear, insecurity, and shame. But the Spirit of God transforms your thinking, breaking the cycle of defeat and replacing it with truth.

Much like healing, renewal is not a one-time event; it's a daily practice. Every morning, you can trade toxic thoughts for thoughts that speak about life. Instead of "I'm not enough," declare, "I am more than enough in Christ." Instead of "This will never change," remind yourself, "With God, all things are possible."

A renewed mind is a healed mind, and a healed mind leads to a healed life. When your thoughts align with God's truth, peace settles in, clarity emerges, and your faith grows stronger.

Prayer:

Lord, I surrender my thoughts to You today. Replace every lie with Your truth. Renew my mind with Your Word so that I can walk in freedom, clarity, and faith.

Journaling Prompt:

Write this sentence and complete it honestly:

"The thought I repeat most often when I'm stressed or discouraged is…"

Then write three short lines beneath it:

- **When this thought shows up, it makes me feel:** (anxious, ashamed, stuck, overwhelmed)

- **The truth I'm choosing to practice instead (Romans 12:2) is: "________________________."**

- **One situation today where I'll practice the new thought is: "________________________."**

Close with this grounding statement:

"I don't have to believe every thought I think. I can choose thoughts that lead to peace."

Act of Self-Love:

Choose one Scripture or truth statement that directly counters your recurring thought.

(Example: *"I am not failing; I am learning."* / *"God is still working."*)

Write it on a notecard or save it as a note on your phone.

Use the 3-times rule today

Read the truth **three separate times**—morning, afternoon, evening.

Each time, pause and take one slow breath.

When the old thought appears, don't argue with it.

Simply say:

"That's the old pattern. I'm practicing a renewed mind."

Then reread the card once.

This trains your brain to **interrupt automatic thoughts**, replace them with truth, and build new mental pathways—one repetition at a time.

Suggested Worship:

"Lord, I Offer My Life" – Don Moen

Journal Entries

Day 25

Day 25: Those Who Wait on the Lord

Isaiah 40:31 (NKJV) – "But those who wait on the Lord shall renew their strength; they shall mount up with wings like eagles; they shall run and not be weary; they shall walk and not faint."

Word of the Day:

Wait

Affirmation:

My waiting is not wasted. As I wait on the Lord, my strength is renewed, and I am lifted higher by His Spirit.

Devotion:

Waiting can feel like weakness, but in God's Kingdom, waiting is where strength is born. The delay is not denial—it is preparation. Every moment you wait on Him, He is building endurance, peace, and deeper trust in your heart.

Our culture teaches us to rush—rush decisions, rush healing, and rush results. But God invites us to wait on Him. Waiting is not passive; it is active trust. It is choosing to rest in His timing instead of striving on your own.

When you wait on the Lord, you exchange your weariness for His strength. Like an eagle soaring on unseen currents, you rise higher not because of your own effort, but because of the Spirit who carries you.

God's promise is clear: those who wait on Him will not be disappointed. They will walk through seasons of difficulty without fainting; they will run the race of faith without collapsing, and they will soar above circumstances with renewed perspective.

The waiting room with God is not wasted space; it's where transformation happens.

Prayer:

Lord, help me to wait on You with faith instead of frustration. Teach me to trust You're timing and lean on Your strength. As I wait, renew me from the inside out and give me wings to soar in Your Spirit.

Journaling Prompt:

Write this sentence and complete it honestly:

"The area where I feel most impatient or worn down right now is…"

Then write three short lines:

- **What waiting here makes me afraid of:** (falling behind, missing out, losing control)

- **What this season might be strengthening in me instead:** (endurance, trust, clarity, boundaries)

- **The truth I'm choosing to practice today (Isaiah 40:31) is:**

"Waiting can renew me, not weaken me."

Close with this grounding statement:

"I don't have to force what God is still forming."

Act of Self-Love:

Stop rushing on purpose

Choose a 10-minute window today where you do nothing productive. Set a timer.

Breathe to restore energy

Inhale slowly for 4 seconds, exhale for 6.

Let your shoulders drop. Let your jaw unclench.

Shift the inner dialogue

Say quietly (once or twice is enough):

"I'm allowed to move at the pace of renewal."

End with one grounded choice

After the pause, take **one steady step**—not the fastest, not the biggest.

Waiting doesn't mean stopping life; it means **moving without panic**.

This practice trains your body and mind to experience waiting as **strength-building**, aligning with the promise that renewal comes to those who wait.

Suggested Worship:

"Wait on the Lord" – Donnie McClurkin

Journal Entries

Assessment

(Take a few quiet moments at the end of Day 5. Answer these questions honestly. There are no right or wrong answers — this is simply a snapshot of your thoughts and feelings after you have progressed this far.)

Hope and Readiness for Change

21. What do I most hope to experience through this 30-day journey?

____

____

____

____

22. Am I truly willing to release the things that have been holding me back?

____

23. What am I afraid might happen if I start healing?

____

24. How will I know I'm making progress?

____

____

25. What's one prayer I want to whisper before beginning this journey?

____

____

Day 26

Day 26: Put On Love

Colossians 3:14 (NIV) – "And over all these virtues put on love, which binds them all together in perfect unity."

Word of the Day:

Love

Affirmation:

I chose to walk in love today. Love covers, heals, and unites every part of my life.

Devotion:

I will express love because Christ's love for me has shown me what that looks like.

To put on love is to see yourself the way that Christ sees you. To put on His nature in the way you love and treat others. It is refusing to live with unforgiveness, shame, or anger, and instead choosing to express love in a way that heals and unites. Love is more than a feeling. Love is an action, a choice, and a way of life. When you "put on love," you choose to wear compassion, kindness, and forgiveness like garments that reflect God's heart through you.

Every day we decide, we should strive to put on love because love is the glue that binds all other virtues together. Patience without love feels cold. Generosity without love feels shallow. Forgiveness without love feels incomplete.

This doesn't mean ignoring pain or pretending everything is perfect. It means allowing God's love to be the covering that transforms brokenness into compassion. This will allow you to reflect God's love as you carry His light wherever you go.

Prayer:

Lord, teach me to put on love every morning as intentionally as I clothe my body, even on the days I don't feel like it. Let Your love be my covering, my strength, and my response in every situation. Amen.

Journaling Prompt:

Write this sentence and finish it honestly:

"The situation or relationship where I'm struggling to choose love right now is…"

Then write three short lines:

- **What emotion is actually underneath my reaction:** (hurt, fear, disappointment, exhaustion)

- **What choosing love here does *not* mean:** (ignoring boundaries, tolerating harm, silencing myself)

- **What choosing love *can* look like in one small, healthy way today: "_______________"**

(speaking calmly, pausing before reacting, offering grace to myself, setting a respectful boundary)

Close with this grounding statement:

"I can choose love without abandoning myself."

Act of Self-Love:

Carry the reminder

Write **"I choose love"** on a sticky note or card and keep it visible.

Use it as a pause, not pressure

Each time you see it, stop for one breath and ask:

"What response would lower harm right now— for me and for others?"

Choose one loving action toward yourself first Love starts inward. Pick one:

- soften self-talk instead of criticizing

- take a short break instead of pushing

- say "not right now" instead of overgiving

- forgive yourself for reacting imperfectly

Then choose one outward action (optional)

A kind word, patience, or restraint—**only if it doesn't violate your boundaries**.

This practice trains your brain to associate love with **clarity, regulation, and choice**, not obligation or self-erasure.

Suggested Worship:

"Love Never Fails" – Brandon Heath

Journal Entries

Day 27

Day 27: Ask for Wisdom

James 1:5 (NIV) – "If any of you lacks wisdom, you should ask God, who gives generously to all without finding fault, and it will be given to you."

Word of the Day:

Wisdom

Affirmation:

I will ask God for wisdom daily, and He will guide me generously without judgment.

Devotion:

We live in a world where everyone has an opinion—whether we want it or not—advice from friends and family, and pressure from culture and social media. It is so easy to get overwhelmed when there are so many voices. That's why Scripture says to ask God for wisdom.

God promises that when you ask Him for wisdom, He doesn't scold or shame you. He pours it out freely, generously, and without hesitation. So many of us think that wisdom is about knowing all the answers, but it's about knowing where to turn for the answers. God promises you that when you ask Him for wisdom, He will not condemn you. God's wisdom quiets the noise of confusion, clears the fog of fear, and gives you a peace that only He can give. Starting today, allow His heavenly guidance to direct you in your earthly situation.

Prayer:

Lord, I ask You today for wisdom. Guide my thoughts, decisions, and steps with Your Holy Spirit. Help me to walk in the clarity of Your truth. Thank You for promising to give wisdom generously when I seek it. Amen.

Journaling Prompt:

Write this sentence and complete it honestly:

"The decision or situation where I feel unsure right now is..."

Then write three short lines:

- **What feels confusing or overwhelming about it is:** "________________"

- **What emotions are influencing my thinking:** (fear, pressure, urgency, people-pleasing)

- **The wise next step I'm open to receiving is:** "________________"

Close with this grounding statement tied to James 1:5:

"I don't need every answer right now. I can pause, ask, and move forward with clarity."

Act of Self-Love:

Before one decision today (small or big), stop for **30 seconds.**

Take one slow breath and place your feet flat on the ground.

Ask simply:

"God, give me wisdom for this."

Notice what follows

- a sense of calm
- a clearer option
- a nudge to wait
- a boundary you need to honor

Act on the clarity you receive, even if it's just to pause longer.

This trains your mind to replace **overthinking with discernment** and reinforces the truth that asking for guidance is strength, not uncertainty.

Suggested Worship:

"Sovereign" – Daryl Coley

Journal Entries

Day 28

Day 28: God's Protection

Psalm 91:5–7 (NIV)

"You will not fear the terror of night, nor the arrow that flies by day,

nor the pestilence that stalks in the darkness, nor the plague that destroys at midday.

A thousand may fall at your side, ten thousand at your right hand, but it will not come near you."

Word of the Day:

Protection

Affirmation:

I am safe in God's care. His protection surrounds me in every season of life.

Devotion:

God's protection is not just about shielding you from harm—it's about covering your life with His presence, even when you don't see it.

Most of the time, fear comes when we feel vulnerable or unsure. But Scripture reminds us that if we believe in God, we are never forsaken or alone. He watches over your coming in and your going out—every step, every decision, every moment. His protection is like a shelter in the storm, keeping you safe from harm. He is always working, guarding your heart, your steps, and your future.

God's divine protection does not mean you'll never face trials; it means no trial will ever have the final say. Like Shadrach, Meshach, and Abednego in the fiery furnace, God may not always keep you out of the fire, but He will always walk with you through it.

His angels encamp around those who fear Him (Psalm 34:7). His Spirit gives peace even in danger. His Word builds confidence when anxiety tries to take over. Living under His protection means you are never alone, never unguarded, and never outside of His reach.

Prayer:

Father, thank You for protecting me in ways I see and in ways I don't. Calm my fears and remind me that Your hand is always upon me. Help me walk with confidence, knowing that I am secure in Your loving hands.

Journaling Prompt:

Write this sentence and finish it honestly:

"The situation where I feel most unsafe or anxious right now is..."

Then write three short lines:

- **What I'm afraid might happen is:** "________________"

- **What evidence I have that I've been protected or carried before is:** "________________"

- **The truth I'm choosing to practice today (Psalm 91) is:**

"I can be cautious without being consumed by fear. I am not alone."

Close with this grounding statement:

"I can acknowledge risk and still rest in God's care."

Act of Self-Love:

Physically pause. Sit with both feet on the floor. Place one hand on your chest and one on your abdomen.

Breathe to signal safety. Inhale through your nose for 4 seconds.

Exhale through your mouth for 6 seconds.

Repeat 5 times.

Name the present moment. Quietly say: **"Right now, I am safe enough."**

(You're not denying risk—just orienting to the present.)

On the final exhale, whisper:

"I am safe in His hands."

Do one small thing today that supports safety and stability:

- set a boundary

- lock in a plan

- ask for help

- step away from fear-driven media

- rest your body

This practice trains your mind to shift from **hypervigilance to grounded trust**, reinforcing the truth that protection includes both God's care and wise self-support.

Suggested Worship:

"Safe in His Arms" – Vickie Winans

Journal Entries

Day 29

Day 29: Years Restored

Joel 2:25 (NIV) – "I will repay you for the years the locusts have eaten—the great locust and the young locust, the other locusts and the locust swarm—my great army that I sent among you."

Word of the Day:

Restore

Affirmation:

God is restoring the years I thought were wasted.

Devotion:

Nothing in my life is beyond His redemption. Lost time can feel like the hardest thing to heal. Missed opportunities, broken relationships, or seasons of pain may leave you wondering if it's too late. But God is the Restorer of years. He can redeem what was lost and bring back to life what you thought was dead.

The locusts that Joel spoke of in today's Scripture devoured everything in their path, leaving total devastation behind. Your "locust" may be something different—betrayal, heartbreak, or hardship that robbed you of your joy or peace. Yet God promises not just to heal but to restore the years that were consumed.

Restoration isn't always giving back the exact thing that was lost; it often means God is giving you something better than anything you could have imagined for yourself.

Something more aligned with His purpose for your life. The thing you thought was wasted; the Father has transformed into something wonderful.

God wastes nothing. Every tear, every prayer, every silent night of waiting becomes part of His restoration plan. And when He restores, He also multiplies.

Prayer:

Father, I thank You for being the Restorer. I surrender every season I thought was wasted into Your hands. Redeem my time, my relationships, my heart, and my dreams according to Your perfect plan. Amen.

Journaling Prompt:

Write this sentence and complete it honestly:

"The season of my life I still label as 'wasted' is…"

Then write three short lines:

- **What I lost during that season was:** (time, trust, confidence, direction, relationships)

- **How that season shaped me in ways I didn't see at the time is:** "________________"

- **The truth I'm practicing today (Joel 2:25) is:**

"God can restore meaning, growth, and purpose—even if the outcome looks different than I imagined."

Close with this grounding statement:

"My past is not a dead end. It's material God can still work with."

Act of Self-Love:

Write down one season you've called 'lost.'

Be specific. Name it clearly.

Next to it, write one way restoration could exist now, even if it's indirect:

- wisdom you gained

- boundaries you learned

- empathy you now carry

- strength you didn't have before

- clarity about what you won't accept again

Say this out loud once:

"That season mattered. It did not ruin me."

Do one forward-facing action today

Choose something small that reflects restoration rather than regret:

- clean or organize one small space

- revisit a goal gently

- rest without guilt

- reconnect with someone safe

- write one hopeful note about your future

This trains your mind to move from **rumination to redemption**, reinforcing the truth that God restores not just outcomes—but *meaning*.

Suggested Worship:

"Restore" – Chris August

Journal Entries

Day 30

Day 30: Crowned With Joy

Psalm 126:5 (NIV) – "Those who sow with tears will reap with songs of joy."

Word of the Day:

Healing

Affirmation:

My tears have not been wasted. God is crowning this season with joy.

Devotion:

You've walked through sorrow, but sorrow is not the end of your story. God promises that every tear sown in prayer and pain will one day produce a harvest of joy. Joy is not just a fleeting emotion; it is the crown He places on those who endure, having faith in Him.

Healing does not happen overnight; it's a journey, and along the way, you've endured brokenness, waiting, and surrender. But God never leaves His daughters in a broken place. The same hands that wiped your tears and held you in the valley now lift you into His joy.

The joy that the Father gives is not shallow or temporary; it is deep, unshakable, and birthed from knowing God has been faithful through every season. You once mourned, but you now rejoice. Where you once feared, you now walk in courage.

Let Day 30 be a reminder: your healing is ongoing, but you are not who you were when you began. You are walking healed, and joy will continue to follow you all the days of your life.

Prayer:

Lord, thank You for turning my mourning into dancing and my sorrow into joy. Crown my life with Your gladness and let my testimony bring hope to others who are still sowing in tears.

Journaling Prompt:

Write this sentence and finish it honestly:

"The tears I've shed that changed me the most were during..."

Then write three short lines:

- **What that season taught me about myself is:** "______________"

- **What is different in me now because I survived it is: "______________"**

- **The joy I'm allowing myself to notice or receive today is: "______________"**

Close with this grounding statement tied to Psalm 126:5:

"My pain had meaning. I'm allowed to let joy exist alongside my healing.

Act of Self-Love:

Choose one joyful action that fits your energy today

(laugh with someone, play a favorite song, move your body, enjoy something sweet, mark a small win).

Notice one physical sensation: warmth, lightness, ease, relief.

Quietly say:

"This joy doesn't erase my past—it honors how far I've come."

Afterward, write one sentence:

"Today I noticed joy when ___________."

This helps your nervous system learn that joy is **safe**, deserved, and sustainable—not something that has to be postponed or earned.

Suggested Worship:

"Joy of the Lord" – Maverick City Music

Journal Entries

Post-Journey Assessment: "Where Am I Right Now?"

On a scale of 1–10, rate how much peace you currently feel in each area:

- My relationship with God:

☐ 1 ☐ 2 ☐ 3 ☐ 4 ☐ 5 ☐ 6 ☐ 7 ☐ 8 ☐ 9 ☐ 10

- My emotional well-being:

☐ 1 ☐ 2 ☐ 3 ☐ 4 ☐ 5 ☐ 6 ☐ 7 ☐ 8 ☐ 9 ☐ 10

- My ability to forgive:

☐ 1 ☐ 2 ☐ 3 ☐ 4 ☐ 5 ☐ 6 ☐ 7 ☐ 8 ☐ 9 ☐ 10

- My self-worth:

☐ 1 ☐ 2 ☐ 3 ☐ 4 ☐ 5 ☐ 6 ☐ 7 ☐ 8 ☐ 9 ☐ 10

- My hope for the future:

☐ 1 ☐ 2 ☐ 3 ☐ 4 ☐ 5 ☐ 6 ☐ 7 ☐ 8 ☐ 9 ☐ 10

About the Author

Shantel Ragsdale is a woman of faith, a devoted mother, and a passionate writer who believes healing begins when we choose to trust God, moment by moment. As the author of *Walking Healed*, Shantel writes from a place of lived experience, offering encouragement to those learning how to persevere through pain while holding fast to God's promises.

Born and raised in West Philadelphia and now residing in Georgia, Shantel's heart is to uplift and restore others through honest reflection, biblical truth, and unwavering hope. Her writing reminds readers that healing is not about erasing the past, but about moving forward with God, fully anchored in His Word and His love.

www.ingramcontent.com/pod-product-compliance
Lightning Source LLC
Chambersburg PA
CBHW071426300726
48976CB00004B/1249